RESCUED BY THE ORC ENFORCER

VILLAINS DO IT BETTER

KATE RUDOLPH

Copyright © 2024 by Kate Rudolph

All rights reserved.

No part of this book may be reproduced in any form or by any electronic or mechanical means, including information storage and retrieval systems, without written permission from the author, except for the use of brief quotations in a book review.

CHAPTER 1

THIS ONE WAS PERFECT.

Meda scanned the brochure, making sure it answered every single possible point of contention. Safety? Trusted, vetted guards were supplied by the company. Cost? Not the cheapest option out there, but not extravagant. And extra money meant the company wasn't skimping. Time? Six months. A blink of an eye for a twenty-four-year-old.

"You have to work," she whispered to the brochure, tracing her fingers over the picture of the smiling human looking out over a gorgeous vista on an uninhabited planet.

"What's that?" Nebulon Rossi, Meda's father, walked into the sitting room, and she nearly fell out of her chair in shock. Her dad wasn't supposed to be home for another few hours. He was off on business, whatever that meant, and he'd been clear she had to stay indoors.

As if she'd ever be in danger in Crimson Enclave. Her father basically owned this town.

And that was the problem.

In Crimson Enclave she was as safe as any person could be. She could walk down the grungy streets decked out in gold and no one would touch her. Not that her father allowed her anywhere near the seedier parts of the Enclave. No, she was always stuck in the Silver District with its fancy shops and refined clientele. They kept anyone who couldn't afford to live in the Silver District out, and fighting, violence of any kind, was strictly prohibited. Along with drinking, sex shows, cage fights, cursing, and spitting.

Meda had spent her whole life in the Silver District except for small glimpses she caught of the wider world when her father let them travel to their compound in safe, country territory.

And, of course, the times she'd managed to sneak out. She was twenty-four years old. She wanted a life, not this prison of silver and gold.

Still, Meda was tempted to hide the brochure. A part of her wanted to run and run forever, until she was so far out of her father's reach that she could truly be free.

But that wasn't what she was asking for. Really,

all she wanted was something her father had done at her age: a tour around the star system.

If he'd managed it as a young man, why couldn't she?

With fingers she was proud to say didn't tremble, she handed the brochure over to her father. Nebulon Rossi was an imposing man. Tall, broad-shouldered, and with a gaze that could make a the most dedicated lawmen turn and run. He had the same black hair as hers, though his was beginning to go gray at the temples. He let it. But there were no signs of wrinkles, no other hints of age. Her father, she knew, took as many anti-aging treatments as her mother and expected to live well into his hundreds. But the gray made him look distinguished.

Meda had inherited her mother's green eyes and olive skin, and her curly, frizzy hair. Though Meda's mother never let the frizz get to her. Meda sat in the salon chair when she had to, but she'd be there every day for months if she truly wanted to get rid of all her flaws.

She'd rather think about her tour. About freedom.

Her father studied the brochure with a look that turned from curious to stormy.

Meda needed to get ahead of this. "There's plenty of security, all of it vetted. And there are testimonials from several families from the Enclave, so there's not any loyalty issue. And it's six months, so I'd be back before my birthday. You've seen all of these places. Now it's my turn."

Her father didn't glare at her. Meda had never suffered under his angry gaze. But the way he looked at the brochure made her want to shrivel up and die anyway. "Your wedding is next month." He said it like it was a reminder.

It knocked the breath out of Meda's chest. "I already said no. I'm not marrying that man." Kronos Moretti was a business partner of her father's. He'd shown up in the Enclave some time ago and started making a name for himself. A name that was mentioned even in the Silver District. Violent. Cruel. Twisted. He'd be a tyrant over his wife.

Meda wouldn't be that woman.

"Perhaps he will allow you to take this tour as a wedding present," her father said as if she hadn't said a word. "I'll bring it up to him."

She wanted to yank the brochure back and keep it safe. "I'm not marrying Kronos," she repeated. She hated the way her voice went high and desperate, like she needed her father's permission to refuse a marriage.

"Andromeda ..." her father sighed. "This isn't up for negotiation. Kronos has been nipping at my heels for the past six years. He controls enough territory bordering mine to be … an issue. And he wants you to make an alliance. It's time you helped your family for once instead of taking my money and spending it on everything in the District that catches your fancy."

He didn't raise his voice, but the words cut deep into her. "Father—"

"I've given you months to come around to this idea. Your mother has set up an appointment for your dress. You will go with her, and you will choose what you want. You can be involved in the wedding planning or not, but you will show up for the ceremony, and you will say I do when the magistrate prompts you." His words were hard, but his face softened. "Kronos wants this alliance too much to risk angering you. I've known him to be reasonable. Once your marriage is secure, he'll allow you to go on this or any other tour you wish, so long as you belong to him."

Belong to him.

Her stomach roiled. She didn't want to belong to anyone but herself.

But that was already a lie, wasn't it? Meda belonged to Nebulon Rossi as long as she lived in his house. And her world would always be as small as the Silver District's borders. Her father could make as many promises as he wanted, but she doubted that Kronos would let her leave the planet.

Would he even let her leave her house?

Men in her father's line of work—those who controlled the city, however that worked—didn't stay in power by letting their wives and mistresses do anything they wanted. If he ruled his territory in the city with a cruel hand, there was no reason to think his home would be any different.

Though a small part of Meda wondered if that was true. She heard whispers about her father, too. He'd risen to power before she was born. He'd bathed in the blood of his enemies and killed innocents if the rumors were true. And he loved her as much as any father could. Didn't he?

He still wanted to sell her to a violent man.

"Please, sir, I'm not ready. What if I went on the tour and then married Kronos?" The words were acid on her tongue, but Meda would figure something out later. As long as she could delay the wedding, everything would be okay.

Any softness on her father's face dissolved, and he crushed the brochure in his palm and let it drop. He took two swift steps toward her, and Meda backed up, her heart pounding. Her father had never laid a hand on her, and she knew he never would. But she could see how close he was to losing his temper.

"Now is not the time for tantrums, you spoiled

girl." He grabbed her wrist and tugged her towards the door. "Go to your room, right now, and stay there until I summon you. You can consent to this marriage and make it pleasant, or I will drag you there myself, and there will be no talk of Grand Tours for a very long time." He shoved her into the hallway, and Meda stumbled, catching herself before she fell.

Her father slammed the door shut, and Meda stared at the red marks on her wrist. It might bruise, but it wasn't the pain that brought tears to her eyes and made a sob catch in her throat.

If her father, the man who loved her, the man who always said he had her best interests at heart, could say those things to her, what would a brute like Kronos Moretti do?

Meda scrambled to her feet and took the stairs two at a time. Without giving herself much time to think about it, she grabbed a duffel bag out of her overstuffed closet and started pulling clothes off the hangers.

She couldn't marry Kronos. She couldn't let her father break her will.

She had to get out of there.

CHAPTER 2

THERE WAS blood on Vorok's knuckles. He looked down and let out a heaving laugh at the asshole on the ground outside of Quantum. Every time the door opened to let one of the dancers out into the alleyway for a break, he heard the pulsing beat of the music and could smell sex and some sweet, smoky drug that gave the whole place a hazy, relaxing feel.

The sign on the main drag of the Red District said Quantum was a place to watch dancers strip down to nothing and where the alcohol was cheap. But on nights like the dancing had a way of turning into sex and, if Vorok was really lucky, the orgy would turn into a brawl. Or the other way around.

Sex and violence—it made the perfect job for an orc.

"You pay," Vorok grunted. And maybe it was a bit of the orc act—all grunts and single syllables, as if he couldn't string together a single sentence. Half the bosses out there hired orcs to bust heads, and they didn't like it when monsters like him mentioned things like working conditions or health care.

Vorok held out a hand, his thick green fingers sticking out of the fingerless leather glove he wore. It was torn a bit, but he could sew that back up himself. He'd have to. Nebulon Rossi paid shit for henchman work.

The man whimpered and handed over three credit sticks. Vorok checked the value and shoved them in his pocket before giving the would-be thief a final kick to the ribs and sending him on his way.

The violence did little to settle him. That was happening more and more these days. Vorok had been busting heads in the Crimson Enclave for years now, and as the head bouncer at Quantum, he'd risen higher than most orcs ever managed. Despite the seediness, Quantum was one of Rossi's most profitable businesses, and it needed thugs like Vorok to keep things running smoothly. Sometimes it even felt like honest work.

He grunted out a sour laugh. What use did a coward like him have for honest work? For a moment, his brother's face tried to surface in his mind, but Vorok pushed it down with more force than he'd used against the human. His brother was living a life Vorok never could, happy out in the Ravages with their tribe.

Alive.

Vorok's biggest shame.

He needed a drink. Or to take a drag of whatever the girls smoked when they went out there, anything to take the edge off.

No. What he really needed was a fight and a fuck, something long and hard and deep that would pierce through this weak veil of civility he was forced to wear in the city. The leather of his jacket was too tight just then, and he wanted to rip it off with a roar.

He dragged in deep breaths of dirty air and forced himself to calm down before he went into Rut.

With the credits he'd pocketed, he could pay one of the ladies inside to take care of him after her shift. Was the money supposed to go into the club's coffers? Sure, but he'd taken more than the thief owed, and no one had to know if he was pocketing a little bonus. Everyone did it, and Vorok had never been special.

He was a bit more settled now with the plan in mind and the surety that someone would take care of his dick. He had to get back inside. It would be mayhem if he was gone for too long. But despite the ever-present sour smell in the air, the night was pleasant. It was early spring and still cool enough that someone with thinner skin might have needed a thick jacket. The moon shone brightly overhead, barely dimmed by the glowing neon of the city all around him.

A part of him longed for the open fields of home. He could be running right now, hunting a boar or a bear, something that gave a good fight and died an honorable death. He could have a mate at home, or maybe even hunting beside him. He could satisfy himself in her heat and fall into Rut whenever he wanted.

But none of the women in his village would take him. No, he'd probably be killed on sight.

He deserved it.

With thoughts of the Ravages trying to pull him under, Vorok turned back towards the club. But something made him pause.

"This isn't where I told you to take me," a woman's voice cut through the night. Awareness shot up his spine, his cock twitched, and he sucked in a harsh breath. There was something familiar about that voice.

He heard a taxi door slam and then an outraged cry. "F ... f ... forget you!" she yelled.

Vorok had to bite back a laugh. Anyone who

stumbled over a simple fuck had no place in the Red District. He knew he should leave her be. Someone would come along before long and rob her of every last cent. She was probably some spoiled Silver District lady trying and failing to slum it.

But Vorok's mood was shifting into something almost kindly. He could get her a ride back home and call it his good deed for the … he wasn't actually sure when he'd done his last good deed.

He lumbered out of the alley and froze.

That wasn't any Silver District princess. It was *the* Silver District princess. Andromeda Rossi. Nebulon Rossi's treasured child.

And the object of more than one of Vorok's dirtier fantasies.

She had no idea who he was, he was certain. He'd been tapped to do perimeter security the last time the family had taken to their compound on the border between the city and the Ravages. That was the first time, the only time actually, that he'd seen Meda Rossi. And one look at her had speared him like a boar's tusk. If a boar's tusk could make need thunder through him.

Dark curls had haloed an expressive pale face as she tilted her head up to soak in the clear sunlight. A tight, black swimsuit hugged her ample curves, and a rainbow-colored, shimmery sarong had hung off her hips, tempted him to march over and strip it off. Or wrap her up so no one but him could see. Vorok had seen beautiful women before, women who knew how to use it like a weapon, but none of it had affected him the way Meda Rossi had.

Then she'd noticed him looking and offered him a kind smile, rather than the "haul off, orc scum," he expected from rich humans like her. No, not like her. No one was quite like her.

She'd become his quiet obsession in the months since.

He didn't see her often. Nebulon Rossi kept her locked up tight in the Silver District. But there were always whispers about the boss's daughter. And when there weren't whispers, Vorok had his fantasies.

In none of them was she standing at the mouth of a dingy alley in the Red District waiting to get robbed … or worse.

This was no place for an innocent girl like her.

Meda's gaze landed on him, and her expression shifted from frustration to recognition, and for a moment, she smiled. Then that recognition turned to fear, and she ran.

Vorok chanced a glance down the alley to see who she might have been smiling at, but there was only him. No way she would have recognized him after one pleasant exchange. It didn't matter anyway.

He took off running after her, leaving the club to its own devices. Rossi would kill him if anything happened to his daughter. Vorok chased Meda through the streets, her duffel bag bouncing against her hip as she ran. She was surprisingly fast for a pampered Silver District princess.

Three turns of three corners, and Vorok lost sight of her, but he had the advantage of orc speed and endurance. His senses would have been heightened out in the Ravages, but the city overwhelmed him with the smell of piss and worse. Still, he picked up her trail.

Meda Rossi was clever; he'd give her that. She zigzagged through the streets, ducked into alleys and behind buildings like she actually knew the Red District, and Vorok was almost impressed.

But orcs were hunters, and she was his prey.

He cornered her in a dead-end alley, and Meda's eyes widened, her gaze darting around wildly for some sort of escape. There was none. This alley was one of the Red District's traps, made so bad guys like him could catch good girls like her and do whatever they wished.

Lucky for her, all he wanted to do was send her home.

No, that wasn't all he *wanted*. But it was what he was going to do. In his dreams, this chase could end some other way, but tonight, he had to do the right thing. He snorted out a sour laugh. Since when did he care about what was right?

Meda turned her gaze to him, seemingly resigned to the fact that she was trapped. "I know you," she said.

"I'm not going to hurt you." His words came out more like a grunt from between his tusks. When his blood ran hot and the hunt was on, they extended farther from his jaw than usual. Normally they were barely noticeable. Right then he might have looked like a monster. He didn't want her running again. "I saw you get out of the taxi. Let's get you home."

Meda's hand slipped from where it was clutching the duffel bag, and she had to reposition. She must be nervous. "I'm not going back there." Her voice was steady, even if the hand he could see shook.

Ah, a bit of rebellion. How old was the girl? Twenty? A bit older? Orcs grew to adulthood faster than humans, a necessity for survival in the Ravages, but he knew Meda was all woman and fighting against the reins of her father's control. Lying would be his best option here. Tell her he'd help and lure her back. Rossi might even reward him if he found out.

Instead, Vorok hesitated. "Did he hurt you?" He'd

seen Rossi flay a man once. The asshole had almost deserved it, but that kind of refined bloodshed made Vorok's stomach turn. Give him a brawl any day; he wasn't a surgeon of violence.

"No!" Meda shrank back and then straightened. "He's never hit me." Her eyes flicked down to her wrist, but it was covered by her dark jacket. She gulped, her throat working against the words. "He's forcing me to marry Kronos Moretti."

Vorok couldn't have stopped the curse that came out of his mouth if he tried. "He'll kill you." He'd seen what Kronos did to the whores he bought. A delicate wife wouldn't stand a chance.

Meda's eyes widened in hope, and she offered him a smile. "I'm just trying to get to Ombra. I can catch a flight there, get off the planet."

"You think your dad doesn't have people on Ombra?" It was a space station in geostationary orbit above Crimson Enclave, their lifeline to the rest of the system. "You can't throw a stone without hitting someone in his pocket up there."

"Really?" She slumped again, and Vorok's own heart twisted.

But what could he do? She belonged to his boss, and he had to return her if he wanted to keep the skin on his back. And he meant that literally. He took a step forward and held out his hand. "I need to take you back home. Try and stall the marriage. I'm sure Kronos will do something to piss off your father soon enough, and the whole thing will get called off."

He doubted it was true, but they'd come to the lying portion of this interaction. He had to get her out of there, and even if he felt bad about it, he had to take her home.

If he didn't do things just because he felt bad about them, he wouldn't have a job.

He took one step closer, and Meda flinched.

The next thing Vorok knew, his whole body lit up with electric shock as she pulled a taser out of her bag and pulled the trigger. He collapsed into a helpless pile of orc meat, unable to do anything but groan. Meda took her chance, darting past him, but he managed to reach his hand out and wrap it around her ankle.

She went down.

Vorok managed to crawl over her and pin her beneath him, but his body still hummed with the electricity and something else.

Pure lust.

His cock hardened painfully, and it took every ounce of control he had not to rut against her. That move there was what an orc woman might have done in a mating dance, though an orc woman would use her fists.

His little human had fire in her.

Vorok made a split-second decision, ignoring the fact that it might be his last. He grinned down at Meda. "You've got spirit, little human. Come with me, I'll get you off this planet."

She glared up at him. "I'm not an idiot."

He heard something in the distance and forced himself to look away. They were still in the dingy trap of an alley, and it wouldn't take long for someone to find them. He sprang to his feet and offered her a hand. "We're deep in your father's district now," he said. "And if anyone finds us, they'll kill me and take you back without asking questions. Or worse, one of your father's rivals will find you. Or Kronos Moretti. No one out here is going to help you. Except me."

She got to her feet, ignoring his hand. "Why?"

He couldn't tell her it was because his cock was throbbing so hard he might go mad with it. "I said it already, I like your spirit."

"You work for my father." She wasn't backing away. He was still between her and the mouth of the alley, but he had her full attention.

"There's no such thing as loyalty in Crimson Enclave, baby. I don't give a shit about your father. But you're interesting."

He could see her mind working. She didn't say it,

but they both knew that what he'd said was a double-edged sword. If he had no loyalty to her father, he had no loyalty to her. There was nothing stopping him from locking her up somewhere and selling her to the highest bidder. Maybe with someone else, Vorok would have considered it.

He wanted something else from Meda.

He couldn't have it.

But he could help her.

"I hear a patrol getting close," he warned her. He wished he was lying. If they didn't move soon, they'd have to fight their way out.

Meda waited another eternity of a moment before giving a decisive nod. "Fine. Get me out of here."

They ran.

CHAPTER 3

MEDA WAS MAKING the biggest mistake of her life for the second time today. Vorok ran so fast for someone so big. Orcs had been a bit of an obsession of hers for a short while when she was a teenager. She'd begged her father to let her go along with a research mission into the Ravages and had been denied again and again. That one was probably for the best, she'd admitted to herself after a few years of pouting. Not every research mission made it back out intact.

Her father thought of orcs as simple brutes, she knew. Most of the rulers of Crimson Enclave did. They were big, and they fought like monsters. But orcs were just as smart as humans, they had societies just as complex. And there was even a school of scientific thought that orcs and humans shared a common ancestor. Though she wasn't sure if she agreed with the space progenitor theory of evolution.

Not the time to get caught up in the science.

She was sucking in deep breaths every time Vorok paused to check their path. They'd stuck to alleyways and side streets, and she was thoroughly lost by now. She'd thought she knew the Red District well enough after the few times she'd snuck in and all the maps she'd studied. Now she was realizing she'd never been more than a tourist. Vorok knew this place like it was his home.

It was. Obviously. Where else would he live?

"Why do so many orcs live in the city?" she asked while they were ducked in a shadowy corner waiting for the path to clear. "I thought orcs loved nature."

Vorok gave her a strange look. "You think all orcs are the same? Don't humans like nature too?"

Point taken. Meda didn't follow up. Maybe an orc used to bashing heads for her father wasn't the best source for information on his species. "Are you sure we can't go to Ombra? There's a flight leaving in two hours. I still have time to make it."

Vorok growled, and it did strange things to her body. She pressed her legs together and breathed through her mouth, trying to ignore the reaction.

"They'll stop you at the planet side transfer

station. You won't even get up to the space station." He spoke with a certainty that made her depressed.

"Then how can I get off the planet? I don't exactly have a spaceship." Could she steal one? How hard would that be? Meda dismissed the thought as quickly as it came. She didn't know how to pilot a ship. She'd just as likely crash it. "I *need* to get off this planet." The longer she stayed, the more likely it was that her father or Kronos would find her. She wouldn't escape a second time. It had only worked this once because her father didn't expect it.

"Ombra's not the only space station above Syndica," said Vorok. "Your dad doesn't have any influence over Astra."

She scoffed. "Yeah, because Astra is on the other side of the freaking continent above a city ruled by his enemies."

Vorok just stared at her.

Oh. Right. That was a good thing.

"How do we get to Nocturna?"

"I'm working on that," Vorok muttered. Then he grabbed her arm and hauled her out of their hiding spot. She expected another run, but they didn't go far this time.

Instead, he opened the door to a small apartment building and ushered her inside and up a rickety flight of stairs to a door that didn't have any visible number or other way to mark it. She didn't even see a lock.

Vorok placed his hand on the center of the door, and the nearly invisible bio-scanner lit up and the door opened with a click. "It's keyed to me, so if you try to leave, you'll be locked out," he warned.

The lights came on, illuminating a small room. There was a kitchenette, a bed that dominated most of the rest of the room, and a door Meda assumed led to a bathroom. It smelled a bit like orc, like Vorok, slightly wild and unrestrained, and she shivered.

"Home sweet home," Vorok muttered.

"This is where you live?" Meda couldn't keep the judgement out of her voice.

He turned and growled at her, his tusks jutting farther out of his mouth. "We can't all live in palaces, princess."

Now wasn't the time to point out she lived in a townhouse, not a palace. It was palatial enough compared to this. But surely her father should have paid enough for Vorok to afford ... more.

There was nowhere to sit except for the bed and a huge stool that was shoved up next to the counter in the kitchenette. Meda chose the stool and teetered precariously for a moment, her feet dangling. "So, what's the plan?"

Vorok jabbed a finger at her. "You stay here and

don't cause any more trouble. I need to go and get us transport out of here."

"A ship?" Flying vehicles were forbidden to fly over Crimson Enclave except for delivery drones and low altitude bikes.

He huffed out a sardonic laugh. She didn't know orcs could be sardonic. "We'll see what I can get. Probably a bike. I've got a guy. But the longer you're on the street, the more likely we are to get caught."

"You want to take a motorbike through the Ravages?" Maybe he didn't see the danger since it was his ancestral home and all, but Meda knew that expeditions always went in heavily armored vehicles. It was the only way to stay safe from orc hunters and the even scarier beasts that lived out there.

"Don't get scared now, girl."

"I'm not a child," she snapped. She wouldn't be in this mess if everyone could acknowledge that she was a woman in control of her own life.

Vorok stalked closer until he loomed over her, presence unyielding. This close, it was clear he was big. Big enough he could wrap one of those hands of his around her throat and squeeze until she breathed no more. She should have been afraid. But there was something about his presence that called to a deep darkness within her. Yes, her heart rate sped up. But it wasn't in fear.

"Believe me, princess, I know you're no child." He leaned in close and breathed deep.

Why did that make her shiver?

He grunted and stepped back. "I'll be back before sunrise. Don't go anywhere. You'll be safe here for a bit."

"You want to just leave me here?" She was off the stool now and right up in Vorok's face ... or, well, his shoulder. She'd need a step stool to get any higher. "What if he finds me? I thought you said you'd protect me!" She hated how high her voice went, how desperate. She shouldn't be trusting Vorok at all. In fact, she knew she should run the second he left her alone. But he'd caught her so easily she feared that it would happen again. And the next guy who caught her wouldn't be so nice.

Unless this was all a trick, and he was going to get her father.

"What's that look for?" Vorok's hand hovered near her face and froze there for a moment before he lowered it.

Had he been about to touch her? Would she let him?

Did she have another choice?

"If I wanted to turn you over to Rossi, I wouldn't have bothered to bring you here," the orc said plainly. "Same goes for if I was going to turn you over to anyone else. It's tougher than an orc hound's balls to hide you in the city, but I'm doing it anyway. So, wait here. Yeah?"

Should she lie? Should she stay? Could she trust Vorok?

"Why are you helping me?" She had to know.

"I told you already." He was getting frustrated now. He turned away, making to leave.

Meda placed her hand on his arm. The thick leather of the jacket kept her from touching his skin, but heat radiated off him, so unexpected it burned. For some reason, she thought he'd be cool to the touch.

Vorok looked down at her hand and sucked in a breath.

"Why are you helping me?" she repeated.

He jerked his arm away. "Next time you touch me, princess, I'd prefer your hand on my cock." Then he stalked out of the apartment and let the door slam behind him.

Meda stared at it for several seconds, imagining him walking down those stairs and out onto the streets below. She could get away now. If she was smart, she would. Instead, she couldn't stop staring at her hand, as if that fleeting touch had scarred her to the bone.

Stupid, spoiled females. Vorok let the curses roll around in his head as he stomped through the streets. They'd be missing him at the club by now. Maybe. But orcs had a reputation for walking off in the middle of jobs. Vorok had spent years fighting against it, but now he'd use it to his favor.

It wasn't like he could come back after this.

Was he making a mistake?

A bit of rough play, and he'd been putty in the princess's palm. If she tried it again, he might actually beg her to be his mate. She couldn't know that weakness. An orc would understand, but she was very much *not* an orc.

He could still smell the floral scent of her and wondered if that fleeting touch had transferred some of her fragrance to him. Or was he already so far gone that she'd burrowed into his nostrils, a reminder for every moment he wasn't with her?

He was a fool.

But he'd made his choice, and there was no going back now. If the boss found her in his apartment, he'd cut off Vorok's balls before he flayed him alive. Then it would be his head. There was no way to go but forward.

Luckily, there was one other person in the city he

could trust a little. Not with the whole plan, of course, but Gornak might help. Even better, the orc bastard owed him a pile of favors.

It was time to collect.

Gornak didn't work for one of the human crime lords that called Crimson Enclave home. Instead, he was a member of a gang of orcs who rode monster-cycles and terrorized the outer edges of the city. They hired out to anyone who had the credits, and they weren't afraid to get bloody.

If Gornak realized who Vorok had hiding in his apartment, this would go bad fast.

Vorok strolled up to the Orc Fire Monster-Cycle Club and took the place in. They'd redecorated. Or maybe they hadn't bothered to clean up the blood from the last brawl. The place was dark wood and black steel. It wouldn't have looked out of place in the Ravages, and Vorok was sure that was on purpose. Orc Fire didn't want anyone to forget where they'd come from.

There was a bar in the back of the club, but the booze was locked away behind thick plasglas, and no one was there to serve.

At first, Vorok thought the place was empty, though it would have been locked up if no one was there. Then there was a screech as one of the tables was righted, and Gornak stood up.

They were from different tribes. Gornak's people came from farther southwest on the continent, and his skin was a brighter green. He wasn't wearing a shirt at the moment, and one of his arms was covered in black tattoos he'd received before he made his way to the Enclave. The other arm was covered in ink he'd gotten in the club.

"You're a long way from home," Gornak grunted when he saw Vorok.

No use telling the guy that his apartment was only a few blocks away. Vorok liked his privacy. And it was a lot harder to attack a man at home if you didn't know where he lived. "The raid on Moretti's place. That truck of Rossi's that disappeared. The fire at the Gravity Club." All times that Vorok had covered for Gornak or his club in the last couple of years.

"I cut you in on that shit," Vorok reminded him with a scowl.

"And you promised me a pile of favors. I'm calling that in." When Gornak made those promises, Vorok had assumed they'd just hang over their friendship until one of them got killed. He hadn't imagined he'd flee the city with his boss's daughter. "I need a bike. A GX1400, maybe an RT2000. Something like that."

Gornak raised his eyebrows. "Those are big bikes. Heavy duty."

"I'm a big guy." He stared Gornak down as he said it, ignoring the fact they were nearly the same size.

Gornak shrugged. "I got a shipment coming in next week. I can get you something."

"I need it tonight. Now." He didn't want to stay in the city a moment longer than necessary. Soon enough, they'd be looking for Meda. They needed to be far away when the search started in earnest.

Gornak laughed, a deep guffaw that came from his belly. "I can't magic up a bike. Everyone's away on business right now."

"Then give me your bike." He'd take what he could get. But this request was taking him a bit too close to desperation. Asking an Orc Fire MC member for his bike was like asking for his child. Only more important.

A contemplative look fell over his friend's face as he looked Vorok up and down. "What shit have you got yourself into this time? No, don't tell me. My knee is still acting up from the last time I was involved in your schemes. You can't have my bike— and not just because I won't give it away for all the credits in the city," he added when Vorok was about to interrupt. "I got in a bit of a jam a few days ago. It's in the shop. Which is why I'm not out on business with the guys right now."

"Then tell me where to get a bike." If he couldn't get a vehicle free and clear from Gornak, he'd have to steal one. And that might call too much attention down on him.

Gornak thought for a minute. "You want a drink?" He nodded back to the bar and walked over, no sign of the limp he'd hinted at only moments before. He placed his hand on a palm reader, and the plasglas slid away. He grabbed a bottle from a high shelf and popped off the cap, taking a deep drink straight from the source. He held the bottle out to Vorok.

"I'm good." A drink might have loosened some of the tension between Vorok's shoulders, but he wasn't letting his guard down until Meda was safe.

The orc placed the bottle down on the bar and took a seat on one of the stools, leaning back against the bar to face Vorok. "I can get you something, but it's going to take a few hours. It's the best I can do. You leaving the city?"

He didn't want to even reveal that much, but the type of bike he was requesting was overkill for the streets of the Enclave. He gave a curt nod.

Gornak made a condescendingly sweet sound in the back of his throat. "Aw, is the scary orc in love? You stealing one of Rossi's girls for yourself and taking her into the Ravages to live as a happy little orc bride?"

It wasn't right. It was so far from right it was laughable. But it might have been a little too close to some of Vorok's sappier fantasies about the woman stashed in his room.

"I need to get out of the city," was all he said.

"Meet me at sunrise at the Meadow. You know the spot. This wipes the slate clean, yeah?" He speared Vorok with a glare.

"All clear," Vorok confirmed.

"Then get the hell out of my club. I'll see you in the morning." He took another drink.

Vorok was tempted to stay for that offered drink. If this was the last time he'd see his friend, maybe a farewell wouldn't be so bad. But the temptation only lasted for a moment before he headed back to his apartment. It was a solid six hours until sunrise. The Meadow was at the edge of Orc Fire territory and close to the border of the city. Luckily, it was nowhere near any place that Rossi controlled. He and Meda would need to leave early to scope it out.

But a night's sleep would do them both good. They'd be traveling hard once they had the bike.

The lights were low when Vorok entered the apartment, and his gaze went right to his bed where he spotted a lump where his blankets should have been.

Meda. In his bed.

He had to bite back a groan. This was the stuff fantasies were made of.

Or tortures the dark gods doled out to remind him of what he'd never have.

He left the lights low, but she must have heard him. She sat up and blinked away sleep. Her curly hair was mussed, and she pushed it back with an absent gesture she must have done every day. It was strangely intimate. "You're back," she said.

"I'm back." He shrugged off his jacket and slipped out of his shoes. Normally, he'd strip down to nothing, but the princess in his bed might object. Besides, he was a bit worried they might have to flee in the night, and he'd rather not need to run with his cock hanging out.

"I didn't think I'd sleep. Your bed is really comfortable." She bunched the covers up around her knees.

Yes, definitely a torture from the dark gods to hear Meda Rossi talk about his bed. "Our ride will be ready in a few hours. Scoot over." He gestured for her to move.

Her eyes widened. "What?" She didn't move an inch.

What was so hard to understand? "It'll be a few hours until we can leave the city. I'm going to sleep until then. You're in my bed. Scoot over." There was room enough for two, and he was just enough of a villain to want to sleep beside her, even if he'd never allow himself to touch.

"The floor's right there." Meda grabbed a pillow and dropped it down beside the bed. "And here's a blanket."

He couldn't stop the dark laugh that bubbled out. "Not a chance, sweetheart." He stalked towards the bed and scooped up the pillow and blanket. "You're welcome to sleep on the floor, but I'm keeping these." He reached over her to place the pillow right where he wanted her to sleep.

She sucked in a ragged breath and stared at his throat. Her tongue darted out to lick her lips, and he had to clamp down on every dark urge that told him to take her right there. A woman didn't look at a man like that if she didn't want him, at least in some corner of her mind.

"Your choice, princess." He didn't touch her. He wouldn't.

Her gaze snapped up, and she glared at him. But after a moment, she moved closer to the wall and gave Vorok room to get into his own bed. His sheets smelled of her, and his body reacted, but he turned to his side, facing away from her before she worried he might get any ideas.

They lay there in silence for several minutes. The mattress itself felt tense with everything that wasn't said. But eventually, Meda's breathing evened out, and she relaxed beside him.

Vorok tried to sleep, but her presence was a burning fire of need right next to him, and he realized this little stunt might have been his stupidest idea of the night.

But he didn't get out of bed. And eventually, he surrendered to sleep.

He dreamed of Meda.

CHAPTER 4

VOROK WAS grumpy in the morning. Meda couldn't exactly hold it against him. And she couldn't exactly call it morning. The sun was only a whisper of a promise on the far horizon, and the city hung in suspended animation. The nighttime denizens had all crept home while the upstanding citizens of Crimson Enclave wouldn't dare to come outside until it was the safe light of day.

On the streets, Meda felt exposed, even if no one was looking.

And she felt *aware*. She had every moment since she woke up with a heavy orc arm slung over her midsection like it belonged there. She was trying not to think about just how much she'd liked it.

What she didn't like was being in the city right now. Any moment, this strange spell of silence was going to break, and she and Vorok would be caught. What would her father do to her if he found her? What would he do to Vorok?

She didn't want to find out.

Silence hung heavy in the air, Vorok a looming presence at her side. But she didn't feel unsafe, she realized. The universe seemed to bend around the orc beside her, as if there was no threat of violence as long as he was around.

Which was freaking crazy. He was one of her father's enforcers. He was probably the last person in Crimson Enclave she should trust. But she kept walking right next to him.

They'd come to a blank pad of concrete surrounded by buildings on all sides. It didn't look like much. She spotted pockmarks in the concrete, evidence that there'd once been metal embedded in the ground. Possibly some kind of playground for whatever children were unfortunate enough to live here. But the concrete had been stripped, and now there was nothing.

"Stay here," Vorok said, stashing her near a concrete half-wall that came up to her waist. "If anyone fires a blaster, duck. And if I go down, run."

She didn't want to think about him going down. "I thought you said this guy was a friend."

Her orc didn't respond.

Hers? Meda was going crazy. She didn't know this guy; she couldn't trust him. And she certainly couldn't think about him as *hers.*

In the distance, she heard tires screeching on pavement, and Vorok tensed. "Get down," he ordered.

She ducked, though she wasn't sure how much good a once concrete half-wall could possibly protect her. Her eyes trailed after Vorok until he was out of sight, and then she forced herself to shift her attention to the area behind her. She was near two of the entrances to this sad little patch of the city, the one she'd come in from and one that was a dark, narrow alley that looked designed to trap people.

But Vorok hadn't warned her not to run there. And the alleyway was so narrow that any orcs coming after her would have to come one by one. The way they'd come in led to a wide street with plenty of room for monsters to circle her and cut her off. She'd have to take her chances with the scary alley.

The vehicles were getting closer, the ground practically vibrating with the bass of their speakers. Vehicles didn't naturally make much noise, but she'd heard of some bikers who modified their bikes to roar like monsters. Was that who they were meeting?

Meda counted the seconds until she heard a screech and the rumble stopped.

She wanted to run. Her heartbeat quickened, and her toes curled in her shoes. She could cross the distance to her escape in seconds. She shouldn't be here.

"You came through," Vorok said to whoever had just arrived.

"Don't tell me you're alone." The second voice sounded disappointed. His accent was orcish, but different than Vorok's.

"Sorry to disappoint. This my ride?" She heard Vorok's footsteps as he moved closer to the other orc and farther away from her. But their location was so flat and echoey she had no trouble making out what they were saying.

"It's not like you to leave the job for nothing," the orc insisted.

"Drop it, Gornak."

Gornak laughed. It wasn't a nice sound. "I asked around. None of the whores are missing."

Vorok remained silent.

Meda's ears tickled with a strange buzzing noise. At first, she thought it was all in her head, but then it got louder and louder. Someone was coming. She was about to yell to warn Vorok when he cursed.

"You sold me out?" The low menace in his voice made her shiver.

"You shouldn't have asked for my bike. You know Rossi doesn't let anyone go." There was a low grunt and then the sounds of fists on flesh.

Meda was frozen in place. Should she run and try to save herself? Or try and help Vorok? Whatever she heard buzzing was getting closer, and she knew if it reached them, they wouldn't get out. It wouldn't be hard at all to trap them in this space.

She stood and took in the sight. Vorok was fighting another orc, both of their tusks out as far as they could go, the vestiges of civility sloughing off each of them like dead skin. But the bike was right there, and it was running.

And it had keys. Thank the stars above.

Meda couldn't have hacked a bio-lock in the seconds she had to make her move, but keys made this whole thing simple.

Neither of the orcs had noticed her yet. They didn't notice as she crouch-walked the rest of the way to the bike. They didn't notice as she confirmed it had enough charge to get them out of the city. And they didn't notice when she sat on it and powered it up.

Vorok only realized what was happening as she powered up the speakers and drove straight for him and Gornak. Both orcs darted out of the way, and she swerved towards Vorok's side.

"Get on!" she yelled.

His face scrunched in comical confusion, but he swung a leg over the seat and wrapped his arms around her as she engaged the motor, and they sped off into the lightening day and towards the edge of the city.

"Let me drive!" Vorok yelled at her above the wind.

"Are you crazy? I'm not stopping yet." It had been a while since she'd ridden a bike, and never like this. Her father had humored her with lessons at a racecourse in the Silver District where she'd learned all about the mechanics and driven her vehicle to the edge of its capabilities. But that was a controlled environment. She hadn't had to deal with street signs.

Or pedestrians.

"Watch it!" The words were only a whisper by the time they made it to Meda's ears.

"Sorry!" she yelled back at the man she'd almost run down. But it was too late now.

"Easy there, racer," Vorok warned.

His lips traced over her ear, and Meda had to grip the handlebars hard to keep from reacting. His arms were wrapped tight around her waist. Even the blistering wind of the road couldn't fully get rid of his scent. His presence enveloped her, and it might have been the most delicious torture she'd ever dreamed up.

They cleared the edge of the city, and Meda started to breathe easier. Gornak may have sold them out, but he wasn't chasing them yet. And once they were deep in the Ravages, they'd be safe. Well, safe from forces in the city.

She drove until she could no longer see the high spires from the towers in the Silver District. It would take days to cross the continent, but they needed to stop.

When the bike stilled, she expected Vorok to let her go, but he held on for an extra few seconds. She didn't pull out of the embrace. Then he moved with a jerk and let go of her. She slid off the bike. Her legs were shaky from the vibration of the ride, and she took a moment to stretch them, then walked back and forth a few paces before her muscles could stiffen up.

Vorok had a dark look on his face. "You can drive."

"You thought I couldn't?" She was sheltered, not uneducated. Was the orc really mad about that? Meda was ready for a fight. She'd been riding the edge of adrenaline since she climbed onto the cycle, and it needed an outlet, or she was going to crash.

But Vorok didn't try and fight her. "I didn't think Gornak would betray me. Stupid. Everyone betrays."

Ah. That. Meda wasn't sure what to do. It hadn't occurred to her to ask a single soul for help in her escape. She had a few friends back in the Silver District, but she doubted any of them would risk the wrath of their own families—or Meda's father—to get her out safely. She approached the orc slowly and placed a comforting hand on his back.

Vorok leaned into the touch.

They stood there like that for several moments until he abruptly straightened and turned toward the bike, opening the sleek saddlebag. "We've got food and water. He must have wanted this to look real."

"Or the betrayal was a last-minute decision." She didn't know why she said it, or if it was any comfort to Vorok. He didn't react.

Meda approached the bike for another reason. She started at the front wheel and inspected every inch of it, looking for trackers that could lead her father—or one of his enemies—right to them. She was about to give up when she spotted a strange indentation in the back wheel well. She stuck her hand into the dark housing of the wheel and peeled off the sticker hiding a dark piece of wire with some circuitry attached.

"Tracker." She handed it to Vorok. He crushed it between his fingers like it was nothing.

"We can't stay here for long." His voice was grim.

She'd already known that. It would have been true even without the tracker. "What's the plan?" she asked. They had hours more of sunlight, but they'd need to be safely ensconced somewhere before night-fall. The monsters in the Ravages put the monsters in Crimson Enclave to shame.

Vorok was silent for several seconds, then he turned to survey the foothills in the distance. "I know a place. Your dad is going to want to catch us before we get to Nocturna. There aren't any rules out here, and his enemies have no power. We have to move fast."

"You're not suggesting riding through the night?" Some stories of the Ravages might have been made up, but dangerous beings roamed these mountains and plains, monsters who loved the eat unsuspecting travelers. And the suspecting ones too. Preparation only went so far for protection out here.

"No." Vorok still wasn't looking at her. "But we have a lot of ground to cover. Are you hungry?" He'd shoved the food back into the saddlebag after he'd found it.

"No." Her stomach was still in knots from the ride and from imagining what was out there waiting for them.

"Then climb on. I'm driving."

Meda didn't argue. She wrapped her arms around Vorok and held on tight as they drove into the unknown.

CHAPTER 5

THE RAVAGES WERE BEAUTIFUL. Pictures and videos had never quite captured just how breathtaking it was. Meda only caught it in bits and pieces as she and Vorok sped down a lesser used road up into the foothills. She knew many orc tribes called this area home and wondered if this was where Vorok was from.

She didn't ask. It was probably a sore subject. Or maybe that was a weird assumption, and he visited his family every time he had a break from his job.

No, Vorok didn't strike her as the type. She'd heard that the orcs in the Ravages disdained the orcs in the cities. Of course, most of her knowledge came from whispered rumors in the Silver District and the few books she's managed to devour on the subject.

The sun was hanging low in the sky, shadows

bleeding out from all the trees that surrounded them. Every minute it grew darker, and eventually Vorok had to turn on the bike's headlight. They had to stop. Things hunted these forests, and they needed to hole up for the night. But Vorok had a destination in mind, and he didn't slow, even as day turned firmly to dusk.

The bike would need to recharge soon. Letting it sit still overnight would be sufficient to give them enough power for another day, she hoped.

Finally, Vorok slowed and then stopped. "We're close," he said.

Close to where, she had no idea. They climbed off the bike, and Vorok walked it into the dense woods before stashing it between two trees that almost looked designed to store such vehicles. Probably just a trick of nature.

"There's a cave up ahead. It should be safe." He didn't tell her how he knew, and Meda didn't ask.

They walked the rest of a narrow path, but before they got to their destination, Vorok stiffened and shoved Meda behind him as he fell into a fighting stance.

Orcs materialized out of nowhere, silent as the night and just as deadly. They wore dark leathers, and many had their dark hair braided back, unlike Vorok's hair, which he let fall down around his shoulders. He'd had it tied back on their ride but had let it fall naturally once they began to walk.

One of the orcs stepped forward. His braids were more complex, and he had a piece of red fabric braided into his hair on each side of his head. He said something in orcish that Meda didn't understand. The orcs around them held their weapons high. The orc spoke again.

Vorok responded. She didn't know what he was saying, but he sounded … defeated. Without thinking, she placed a hand on his arm, and he covered it with his own.

The lead orc said something again, his tone inquisitive.

Vorok hesitated. He glanced back at her, face unreadable. Then he looked back to the lead orc and responded.

There was a heavy silence, followed by the lead orc breaking out into a huge smile, dropping his weapon, and rushing forward to clasp Vorok in an embrace.

"It's been too long, brother," he said in heavily accented Syndican. "Bring your mate. We celebrate."

Vorok squeezed her hand, and Meda understood the silent communication. Keep quiet. Don't contradict them.

And don't show Vorok the way her body responded to the thought of being his mate.

The orcs herded them away from whatever cave Vorok had been taking her to and farther into the trees, perhaps a mile away to a lively village full of orcs and even a few humans. The leader, Vorok's brother apparently, kept an arm around Vorok from the moment they stepped into the center of the village and ignored some of the villagers' questioning looks.

She and Vorok were deposited into a small house right at the edge of the village center. The walls were paper thin, possibly actually see-through when there was a light on inside, and there was a huge bed in the center. The only place with any privacy was the small bathing chamber ensconced in the back of the house. The walls were thicker there, and she hoped no one could hear.

The orcs left them alone, but Meda had a feeling they'd be back.

"What's going on?" she demanded the moment they were alone.

Vorok winced. "Keep your voice down. Sound carries from here."

Pieces were trying to fall into place in Meda's mind, and she was doing her best not to let them. Vorok's brother had called her his mate. This house seemed designed to show anyone exactly what went on inside. She'd heard stories of orc mating rituals, and some things wanted to make sense. Meda steadfastly refused to let them.

"Was that your brother?" she whispered now. "Is this your village?"

He nodded toward the bathing suite, and they both entered. It wasn't just for the privacy. Vorok quickly wet two towels and handed one to her. They both had plenty of dirt from the day's travel to wipe off of them. Meda wiped her face and hands, but no way was she cleaning anything that required taking clothes off while Vorok looked at her.

"I was expelled from my village for cowardice several years ago," Vorok said quietly. "My brother leads them now. I made sure of it."

"What? How?" And what did this have to do with convincing these people she was Vorok's mate?

Vorok didn't look at her as he spoke. He sat heavily on the edge of the huge tub, resting his hands on his thighs. "He had a challenger that planned to cheat. I stopped him before he could. It wasn't … honorable. But Karg lived, and that's all I cared about. He was the leader, but he couldn't let me stay after that, not if he wanted to keep the respect of everyone. He should have killed me. It was the right punishment for the crime. Instead, he exiled me and warned every village nearby about my crime. I was instructed that I could only return when my mate accepted me, and I was ready to present her to the village." He still didn't look at her. "If you don't want to go along with it, I'll understand. I don't think Karg will kill me, and I can survive the night. No one will hurt you; I swear it on my life."

This version of Vorok was different from last night, from the man she'd met in the city. Now he seemed … uncertain and a little desperate. And Meda wasn't about to let him fend for himself. "You're rescuing me," she said. "I can rescue you back just a little."

"You don't understand what you're agreeing to," he warned.

She glanced back at the bedroom. "I'm guessing we need to pretend to have sex while a bunch of your former neighbors sit around the fire out there and cheer us on? Am I far off?"

"There's a dinner first," he said, shoulders sagging.

Meda stepped close and tipped his face up to look at her. She cradled his head in her hands and tried not to get lost in his dark gaze. It was harder than she expected. Just standing this close made her heart flutter and made it clear that anything that went on in the bedroom wouldn't be a hardship. "If this is the worst thing the Ravages have to throw at us, we should be thankful." And then some strange instinct had her leaning forward and brushing a kiss against his lips.

It lasted for only a second, and when she pulled back, her cheeks were burning.

Vorok looked like he'd been struck by lightening. His eyes darkened, and his nostrils flared, and he stared at her like she held the key to his destruction. For a crazy moment, Meda thought he might surge forward and grab her, take her right there.

She wouldn't say no.

But the orc turned away, and that was that.

She had one change of clothes in her pack and hurried to put them on. She didn't need to meet the orc villagers in the dirt-stained pants she'd been wearing for the better part of two days.

She felt like a new person in the clean clothes, though they were nothing special: another pair of dark pants that hugged her body tight so no one could grab hold of her and a dark top. She thought she looked a bit like some kind of burglar—all she needed was something to pull over her head to complete the look.

Meda preferred flowy dresses and bright colors. She'd had to dig deep into her wardrobe to find this outfit before she packed her bag. She could have flowy dresses again once she was safe, she vowed to herself. All they had to do was make it through tonight—whatever that entailed—and get to Astra.

This nightmare would be over tomorrow.

And she'd never see her home again.

The thought struck her so hard that she had to sit down on the bed before her legs gave out. Nausea churned in her guts as she realized she'd never talk to her mother or her friends or anyone ever again. She couldn't. The second she made contact, her father would be after her. And she could never talk to him again either.

Maybe Meda was a fool, but she still loved her father. He was still the man who'd taken time out of a very busy schedule to teach her how to ride a motor-bike. He'd checked under her bed for monsters when she was little and promised her that the orcs he employed wouldn't let anyone get near her room so she had nothing to worry about. He wasn't an evil man. Or, if he was, he'd never been evil to her.

Tears threatened to fall, and Meda swiped violently at her eyes. Was she really going to let herself cry about the man who was trying to force her to marry some brute to improve his business?

The tears fell anyway. Apparently, the answer was yes.

Vorok cleared his throat. Meda squeezed her eyes

shut, trying to banish the tears, and looked up at him. He didn't say anything about the state of her, and for that she was eternally grateful. "What? Is it time to go to dinner?" Darkness had fallen outside, and she could hear people beginning to gather nearby. It was disturbing how easy it was to hear them, as a matter of fact, and reminded her of what was to come after dinner.

He was wearing a different shirt. In the city, he'd been in black and leather, the kind of outfit every enforcer wore. Now he wore a loose-fitting, white top that looked to be made of some sort of soft material. His pants were no longer his leathers either, instead he wore darker trousers that hugged his muscled legs. Meda swallowed hard and forced herself not to think about what those legs might look like without pants.

"I'm washing off my things," he said. His voice was gentler, too, as if he was an entirely different man in this village. "Would you like me to throw in your other clothes? I thought I might as well use that bathtub for something."

Meda gave a tight nod and handed over the wad of her dirty clothes. Then she remembered her under-wear were in there and had to choke back the urge to insist she could wash her own clothing. Saying some-thing would only make it weirder.

She listened to the lapping of the water as Vorok swirled her clothes in the soap, and it helped to ground her. She didn't think she'd ever heard a person clean clothes before. At home—at her father's house—she placed her dirty clothes in a chute and they appeared clean in her closet the next day.

A half hour or so later, Vorok had everything hung up to dry in the bathroom and offered her his arm to take her to the center of the village.

It felt like every eye was on them, and she wasn't imagining it. Vorok was the shamed son returning with a mysterious human mate. Well, maybe not *that* mysterious. She counted at least a dozen humans, most of them paired off with orcs of their own. Some of them were tending to children that looked to be a mix of orc and human. They didn't seem to care about any differences. So, no, Meda wasn't attracting attention because she was human.

It was all because she was with Vorok.

There was a place set up for them right beside Karg. The village leader smiled broadly when he saw his brother and gestured for them to sit. A plate of food was put in front of Meda, and she stuffed her face. It had been a while since she'd eaten, and her stomach had suddenly woken up to remember that.

Karg was speaking to Vorok, but mostly in orcish. A few of the villagers offered her kind words in Syndican, but she didn't understand the rest of it. And for that she was grateful. Maybe she was being weak, but she didn't have it in her to speak to these people. Exhaustion was weighing heavy on her as she realized exactly what she was doing.

Was everyone sitting around here expecting to listen to Vorok fucking her?

Well, clearly not everyone. After an hour or so, some families began to drift away, those with children heading out to their own houses. Another hour passed, and all that was left were Karg and a dozen or so other orcs, all of them wearing dark braided necklaces around their necks.

Meda couldn't stop the yawn that forced its way out of her mouth, and Karg noticed.

He nudged Vorok on the shoulder. "You must see to your mate before she falls asleep on you," he said in Syndican. That caused a chorus of laughter among the other orcs. Either they all understood it and had chosen to exclude her by solely speaking orcish or they understood the tone with no need for translation.

Meda's cheeks heated. Yes, she and Vorok had discussed this, but it was still unsettling to know exactly what these people expected. She secretly hoped there might be some way out of this, that they could plead exhaustion and promise to perform another day.

But Vorok didn't try to beg off, and she knew why. This was his ticket to acceptance in his village. Or, at least, it meant he was no longer living under a death sentence. She could give him that much.

Karg and two others, a man and a woman, stood with Meda and Vorok and walked them back to their quarters. Meda worried they might stand outside the door, but once she and Vorok closed the door behind them, she spotted the orcs walking back to the fire.

The room was lit with only a small lamp beside the bed. She wanted to turn it off so there wasn't even a hint of their shadows showing through the paper walls. But there was a large window that looked out towards the fire, and the orcs would be able to see in well enough if they looked anyway. The moon was full overhead. There was no escaping this.

Meda marched toward the bed like a soldier going to war and crawled on, posed on her hands and knees and waiting for Vorok to play his part. She didn't strip. This was fake, there was no reason. "Come on, baby, take me." It sounded fake to her ears, but she hoped the orcs wouldn't notice.

Vorok stood frozen near the doorway, staring at her like she'd spoken another language.

What did he want? For her to slap her ass and

demand he thrust his cock inside her? Meda could be bold, but she wasn't *that* bold.

"Is that how the weak humans in the Silver District take you?" Vorok's voice rumbled with something dark. "A few thrusts and they call it done?" He took a step towards her and pulled off his top.

Meda snapped her gaze to the headboard. Even in the dim light of the room she could make out the contours of Vorok's naked chest, and it sent a pulse of desire right to her core.

"Look at me," Vorok demanded.

She couldn't refuse. Meda dropped to the side and rolled over, looking at Vorok as he stalked closer. He seemed somehow more real in the dark, as if he'd been made for it. And though she knew this was an act, the hunger on his face looked real. Was he that good of an actor? Or did he really want her?

Vorok leaned over and nuzzled her throat. "You're doing good," he muttered. "We need to make this look real." His hand cupped her hip, and Meda arched up towards him without thinking. "Good, that's it."

His praise was even harder to ignore than the look of him. "It would have looked real," she insisted. "Just like you said, a few thrusts and then all done." She'd had a few boyfriends back in the Silver District, and it hadn't been as dire as Vorok seemed to think.

Though there had been a time or two when sex felt more like a chore than something special.

So how was this, something that really was a chore, more intimate than any encounter she'd had to date?

"Let an orc have his pride, princess." His teeth scraped against her neck, and Meda moaned.

Vorok froze. Then he stared down at her. She swallowed. Hard.

"Good," he said again, voice even more gravelly. "That's it."

"Should I ..." She let her leg fall to the side and skimmed her foot up the back of his calf. Hooking it over his hip felt like crossing some sort of line. Maybe the line of plausible deniability. She was on fire with desire. If she got any closer, would she feel that he was just as into this as she was?

"Show me how you moan when you're coming, princess." His voice was pitched just for her, and Meda's moan was real.

At least at first. Vorok's voice was good. It would haunt her sexiest dreams. But it wasn't enough to get her off. She let her voice crescendo into something vulgar that would have made the most experienced whore in the Red District proud. It went on for nearly a minute and was no doubt heard by every orc outside.

Vorok's eyes were dark with desire, and he vibrated with the strain of holding himself back. Meda's restraint was just as taut. All she needed was the tiniest pressure, and she'd snap. She wasn't sure what would happen then.

Her orc's throat bobbed. "They need more than this," he said. "Scent."

Scent? Her nostrils were full of Vorok, and it was making her a little dizzy. Or maybe that was everything. She hadn't had a sip of wine with her meal, but the orc on top of her had her feeling some kind of way.

"I'm sorry," he muttered it, so quiet that surely no one outside could hear it.

Then he undid the laces of his pants and shoved them down. He rolled off of her and gave her his back, but Meda realized exactly what he was doing. Orc senses were stronger than human. And no matter how good their moans were, the orcs would expect more evidence. Evidence Vorok was making one stroke at a time.

She could lie there and let him. She could stick her fingers in her own pants and find a similar kind of relief. But this was her only night with Vorok. Tomorrow, they'd be in Nocturna, and she'd never see him again. She'd never know what it felt like to really *be* with him.

She didn't let herself hesitate. If she hesitated, she'd regret it forever.

Meda rolled to him and reached over his giant back, sliding her hand down his until she just brushed the tip of his cock. Vorok froze. She kissed his shoulder. "Let me," she breathed. "Please."

His shudder was answer enough, but Meda wasn't taking chances. She straddled his back and rubbed herself against him. Now she regretted that she was still wearing her clothes, but if she stopped to take them off, she feared he might come to his senses.

No time for that.

Vorok rolled towards her, and Meda slid her hand fully around his cock, squeezing and pumping as he groaned into the darkness. He was big. She couldn't get her hand fully around him, and that thrilled her and scared her a bit. Could he even fit inside her?

That wasn't what this was about. She wasn't taking him tonight. She was giving him this. She felt powerful as she stroked him, watching his face contort with pleasure, listening to his groans. He bucked into her hand, and Meda had the wild thought that she could ride him, but no, no, this was enough. It had to be.

With a roar, he came, spurting all over her hand

and the bed. Meda didn't let go, didn't stop stroking him until he was finished.

Vorok collapsed back, breathing heavily. Meda stayed where she was, not quite sure what to do next. If previous experience was anything to go by, he'd pass out and leave her to deal with the mess.

But Vorok was different than anyone she'd ever known. And he proved it right then.

Whatever lethargy pleasure gave to other men, it seemed to invigorate him. He pitched his hips up and bucked her off until she was lying on her back. He was wild with need, eyes wide, tusks peeking out. It should have been terrifying.

Meda wanted more.

"Tell me no right now," Vorok demanded, thick fingers going to the clasp of her pants. "If you don't want this, tell me no."

Not a chance in all the hells. Meda helped him undo her pants and get them off. And then he buried his face between her thighs. She cried out as his tongue lapped against her, and Meda wondered if she'd ever been pleasured properly before. No one had ever gone down on her like he was starving, and she was his only meal.

Meda tangled her fingers in his hair and begged for more, for him to go harder, faster. Her fake cries from earlier paled in comparison to the needy whimpers coming out of her now. Vorok growled against her, and Meda screamed his name, unable to stop the sound, unable to stop any of this.

When she came, it was a wave that washed over her, pulling her under and drowning her in pleasure. When the aftershock let her go, Meda was held tight in Vorok's arms. He stroked her hair and kissed her forehead, and Meda couldn't bring herself to let go.

Sleep was an unstoppable force, but before she surrendered to it, she realized her one regret.

She hadn't kissed Vorok properly, and she worried she might never get the chance.

CHAPTER 6

VOROK WOKE EARLY. The scent of Meda enveloped him, and it would take no effort to pull her close and bury himself deep until he forgot where he ended and she began.

Paradise.

But the sun was peeking through the window, and last night was over. The line had blurred at some point, fake turning so very real. Would she hate him for that? If her eyes opened and viewed him with disdain, his soul would crack in two.

He carefully slipped out of the bed and pulled on his trousers from last night. He doubted he'd ever come back to this village, even with the sins of his past no longer hanging over his head, and he wanted to soak up a few final memories.

The stream he'd swam in as a boy was exactly as

he remembered. The rope hung off a tree branch hanging over the water, and he bet it was sturdy enough to hold his weight. Vorok was tempted, but he left it, instead bunching up his pants and wading to his ankles in the chilly, rushing water.

"I thought you'd be here," Karg said, coming out from between the trees. "Since you're not in bed with your mate."

Vorok was a liar and a villain. He'd spent the last decade busting heads and wreaking havoc for men who made this world a worse place. He didn't feel bad for any of that. An orc had to make a living somehow. But this made something in his stomach curdle. Lying to his brother.

The fact that Meda wasn't really his.

He didn't let any of that show as he turned to face his brother. "There's nothing like this in the city."

Karg opened his mouth to say something but reconsidered and offered him a smile. "I'm glad you came back, that you found your mate. I've missed you."

"We're leaving today." He couldn't have this heart-to-heart with his brother without making that clear. Whatever life there'd once been for Vorok in this village had been destroyed when he murdered his brother's rival.

"Yes, I know." Karg leaned back against a rock, the

perfect picture of an orc at home. "I'm shocked you came here at all."

Could he confide in his brother? What if Rossi followed their trail? Good luck to anyone who made it close enough to an orc village to get caught. They'd be torn to pieces.

"You always kept too much to yourself," Karg said when Vorok remained silent. "Know that you'll be welcome back ... even if you have to come back alone."

Vorok couldn't keep his expression neutral. "What?"

Karg held up his hands. "I'm not saying anything. I'm not laying any accusations. And I heard plenty last night. All I'm saying is that you fulfilled the terms of your punishment. You came back with a mate. If, for whatever reason, you had to come back alone, or if you found a new mate—"

"You think I'd replace Meda?" It was fake, he had to remind himself, but he couldn't stop the words from coming out.

Karg shrugged. "You've lived a life I would never dream of. And I realize situations can become more complicated in the city. Trouble enough in Crimson Enclave that you need to make a new life in Nocturna?"

"Something like that." He trusted Karg not to sell

him out, even if Rossi's men made it out of the village alive. It didn't mean he wanted to share every detail.

"Let's get you fed before you leave us. This time I want a fonder farewell."

Vorok followed his brother from the stream back to the mating cottage. Meda was dressed in her dark clothes, and she gave him a nod when he walked in. There were no soft emotions on her face, nothing hinting at what they'd done the night before. Vorok knew his expression was far more open than it should have been, and he hoped she didn't notice. After last night, he felt like a changed man, like something had fundamentally shifted inside of him.

But if everything went according to plan, he'd drop Meda off in a matter of hours and never see her again.

"Your clothes are dry," she told him. "I left them hanging for you."

"Thanks." Karg had gone to fetch them breakfast and given Vorok instructions to meet him at the fire pit in a few minutes. Vorok wasted no time changing into his riding clothes, but he stuck the pants and shirt from the village into his bag. A memory of home. No one would miss them.

Breakfast was a mix of fruits and meat, and he and Meda didn't waste time savoring it. Once they were done, one of the village women brought out a pack filled with food for the road, and he and Karg said their final goodbyes.

Then Karg stepped over to Meda and said something quiet enough that Vorok couldn't make it out. It left Meda smiling, and she glanced his way quickly then away.

He didn't like his brother and his mate ganging up on him.

Except Meda wasn't his mate. He hadn't truly claimed her. There was no bond tying them together. He was her protector and nothing more. He could never *be* more.

The bike was exactly where they'd left it. They stowed their things in the saddle bag, and Meda had to wear her own pack on her back to make room for the food.

Then they were off.

Vorok watched the terrain for threats. They passed into ogre territory at midday, and he could see evidence of them in felled trees that appeared to have been torn up at the roots. He didn't want to fight an ogre today—or any other day—and thankfully they passed through the most dangerous area without incident.

They stopped to eat lunch when the mountains circling Nocturna came into view on the horizon. Meda had thrummed with excitement at the sight, but Vorok warned her they had a long way to go. The land was mostly flat between them, and Nocturna and the mountains were still hours away. It would be nightfall before they reached their destination.

But they would reach it. No matter what Vorok felt about that.

"What are you going to do in Nocturna?" she asked him. They were lingering over the last of their lunch, as if neither really wanted to get back on the bike.

Vorok shrugged. "There's always a job for an ugly bruiser like me in a place like that. Don't worry about me."

"You're not ugly," Meda protested. "And you're more than a bruiser. You don't have to do that."

A part of him wanted to preen and demand she lay out exactly what she found "not ugly" about him. But Vorok was stronger than that. Barely. "What else could I do, then? I'm not exactly built to be a dancer in one of the clubs."

"You might be a great dancer." She smiled, something wicked glinting in her eyes. "You just need to work at a very discerning club."

A laugh burst out of him. "That's what I'll do, open up the first live naked orc revue."

"Now you're thinking!" The laughter subsided.

She was quiet for a moment. Thinking. Then, "I don't know where I'll end up, but—"

"We should go." He had to say it before she got another word out. "Dire wolves roam this area. Even I can't take on a whole pack."

"Vorok—"

"Get on the bike." He put as much gruff command into the words as he could.

Meda frowned and looked at him for a long moment. But she packed up the remains of the food and stored it without another word.

She was about to offer him a space beside her, he knew. He could feel the offer in the air. And he wanted to accept with everything inside of him. Meda felt like a possibility, like something he'd been looking for forever and only just found. But he had no place at her side. He'd bring her down with him and ruin everything.

He wasn't built to be a mate, a proper mate, to a woman like her. And it was best for her if he just let her be. If she felt anything for him, it would fade.

It had to.

The rest of the ride to the city was a tense affair with the aborted offer hanging between them.

A few hours later, they rode through the pass in the mountains that led into Nocturna, and Vorok paid the toll with some of the unmarked credits he'd taken off the last man he beat up in the name of Nebulon Rossi. Something about that felt poetic, though he wasn't sure how.

Astra's terrestrial terminal was near the edge of the city, and he pulled into the parking lot. This was the end of the journey. They'd made it safely.

So why didn't he feel at least a little relieved?

Meda got off the bike and came to stand beside him. Her hair was mussed from the ride, and her dark clothes were dusty with dirt from the trails they'd ridden. She was as gorgeous as ever.

She stared at his face as if she was trying to impart some telepathic message, but he was no psychic. She leaned in the barest inch and then snapped back. "I'm going to find a flight," she said. "Somewhere far away."

"You should." He reached into his pocket and grabbed what was left of the credit sticks. He handed them over. "Here, in case you need more cash."

She looked down at the money and then back up to him. "Aren't you going to need that? I'll be fine, I'm sure."

He didn't pull his hand back. "As I said, there's always work for a bruiser. I don't want to have done all this work only for you to fail because you couldn't afford a flight. Take the money, princess."

She plucked two of the sticks from his palm but

left the third. She checked the amount of credits and slid them into her own pocket. "That should be enough. More than enough with what I already have. So, you keep that."

He wasn't going to argue. The longer they were in the open, the more likely they were to get caught. "Make sure you choose a flight that doesn't bother with checking IDs. A few of the carriers will just want your name, and you can give them a fake. Get out of this system before you start using your real name again. Your father's power only spreads so far."

"I know that, Vorok." She still wasn't walking away. "You could—"

"Don't trust anyone until you're safely on a ship and out of comm reach. Have a nice life, princess." He turned the bike back on and rolled away before the conversation could go on any longer. But he circled the parking lot a few times, just to make sure that Meda made it into the building.

His job was done.

He had a new life to make in Nocturna. And everything in him rebelled at the idea.

He dumped the bike in an area that looked rife with crime. He left the key in the ignition and walked away. Selling the thing might have been the smarter move, but he didn't want to throw up any flags in case anyone started looking for him here. It was far easier to let someone steal it.

Then he found the seediest bar he could and walked in, waving down the bartender and ordering a drink. He stared into the dark liquid for some time, wallowing.

Now that his job was over, now that Meda was safe, he had to face the truth. He didn't want to bust heads. He just wanted her. To hold her, to cherish her.

To love her.

But what kind of life could an orc enforcer give a human princess?

He swallowed down his drink in one gulp and motioned for another. The second one tasted like sour piss coated in fire, and he scowled. Was he really going to sit here all night and get wasted on disgusting cheap alcohol? Was that his life now?

Before he could make up his mind, the door swung open, and he jerked his head around to see who it was. Bikers, by their jackets. He didn't recognize them. This was probably their turf. Maybe he could be like Gornak and join a motorcycle club.

Too bad he'd given up his bike.

The bike.

Fuck.

But realization sank in only a moment before one

of the bikers came up behind him. Something slammed into his head, and everything went black.

CHAPTER 7

THE TICKETS WERE MORE expensive than Meda expected. She had enough credits, barely, but she wouldn't have much privacy for the next week before she ended up at Nebula Outpost, wherever that was. No one had asked questions beyond her destination at the ticket counter, so Meda was on the right track.

She passed into the main part of the terminal where she would take a shuttle up to Astra station. She'd never been in space before, so it should have been exciting.

All she could think of was Vorok.

He could be with her right now if only he'd let her get the damned question out. But maybe he just hadn't known how to let her down gently. Maybe last night had been nothing more than a bit of fun for him.

She'd spent the entire night and today damming up her emotions so none of them leaked out. Trying to ask him to come along with her had felt like pulling out a piece of her soul, but she'd still done it. And it had earned her exactly nothing.

Good riddance.

Except that was a lie. She wanted Vorok. Maybe it was crazy. Maybe it was the excitement of running away. But it felt real with him, more real than anything else ever had.

She was tempted to leave the station and go find him, to demand he acknowledge that there was something between them, that he meant something when he called her princess.

But she stayed put. She'd tried to ask twice, and he'd cut her off both times. He'd made his wants clear. Well, clear enough.

There wasn't much security to get into the terminal, but she was stopped at a turnstile that had two slots: one for ID and one for a credit stick. The perfect reminder that Astra was exactly like home in all the ways that counted.

According to the plaque on the turnstile, entrance was free if she scanned her ID. Walking through without scanning cost five hundred credits.

She had 512 credits left on her remaining credit stick. She could afford to pass through anonymously, but then she'd have twelve credits to get her by for the more than week's journey to Nebula Outpost. She couldn't buy food on that, and she doubted she could rely on the kindness of strangers. She'd probably used up her luck on getting her on Vorok's bike.

Should she have taken the final credit stick he offered? No, it felt wrong to take everything from him.

Meda backed out of the line. She couldn't scan her ID. Even if her father didn't have people looking for her in Nocturna yet, he would soon. Scanning her ID would tell him exactly where she was, and possibly where she was going. She couldn't risk it.

Could she get a fake ID for less than five hundred credits? Could Vorok help with that?

Of course, at the first sign of trouble, she thought of him. No. He'd driven away. He was done with her. She had to fix things herself.

Meda forced herself to think. She had no idea how to get a fake ID, but she could get money. She had it in her accounts, and she'd seen a credit machine outside the building. If she pulled the credits there and her father found out, hopefully she'd still have enough time to get on the ship and be far away before he figured it out. She had four hours to get up to the station and get on her ride off of Syndica.

Surely that wasn't enough time for him to find her.

Decision made, she headed outside the station and got in the line at the credit machine. The person at the front of the line was taking their time, and the three people after him were clearly frustrated. Meda didn't like waiting in the open, but she didn't have another choice.

Several minutes passed, and finally the first person was done. The line had just started to move when she heard tires squeal in the parking lot and a terrified scream.

She didn't have time to look at what was going on before someone slipped a black bag over her head and dragged her away.

CHAPTER 8

MEDA WOKE up in a dark room. She was slumped against a warm, firm form who was groaning softly.

Vorok.

She jolted fully awake and sat up, making him curse. "Princess?" he asked, a note of pain in his voice.

"Are you hurt?" she demanded. It was too dark to see much, and she wanted to run her hands over him to make sure everything was okay. Somehow, she doubted that was the case.

"Some asshole hit me with bat." She could hear the scowl. Then it turned even darker. "Did they hurt you?"

"No, I don't think so. They covered my mouth with something, and I passed out." It had happened after she'd been dragged into the back of a vehicle. Someone had pressed something against the cloth bag on her face, and two breaths later she was unconscious. Then she was here. "Where are we? Who hurt you?"

He groaned again. "Easy there, princess, or someone might think you care."

"Of course I care, you idiot. I've been trying to say that all day!"

The confession hung in the silence between them. Oh, to hell with this. Meda reached out and found the edge of Vorok's cheek. She traced her way until she found his mouth and kissed him with all of her might. He was stiff for a moment, and then his mouth softened, and he groaned into her, kissing her back.

With the taste of him in her mouth, she could pretend they weren't trapped in some dank dungeon with dangerous people no doubt on the way. But she couldn't care about that for the moment. She shifted until she was straddling Vorok's lap and deepened the kiss, desperate to show him everything she couldn't put into words.

Vorok had that same desperation, holding her tight against him and devouring her. Meda tangled her fingers in his hair and rocked against him, but only for a moment.

It was one thing to get off with him with the orc village elders observing from a safe distance. They hadn't meant any harm.

Someone here wanted to hurt them both.

Meda forced herself to pull back, but she didn't slide out of Vorok's lap. "Does that clear some things up?" she managed to ask.

He cradled the back of her head. "Maybe."

She wished she could see his face. This was not a conversation to be had in the dark. But it might be the last chance. No, she had to focus on the problem at hand. "How'd they find you?"

He huffed out a disappointed breath. "Gornak put the word out to the biker gangs in Nocturna. He told them I stole his bike. They found the bike, then they found me. And I'm guessing that once they knew I was here, someone back in Crimson Enclave was able to piece together that you'd be at the transport station."

The lights came on blindingly bright, and the door slid open. Meda didn't recognize the human who walked through the door, and he certainly didn't look like a biker. He wore a dark suit, and most of his face was obscured by a mask and dark glasses. "That's about right," he said in a Nocturnan accent. "They said you were smart for an orc."

Vorok stiffened under her and wrapped her tight

in his embrace, as if he could protect her from the man pointing the blaster at them.

Meda had to say something. "We can—"

"Do not insult me with an offer of payment. Kronos Moretti has more credits than you ever will, and a favor from him is worth even more than that. When he finds out I have his bride and the orc scum who thought he could steal her away, he'll reward me handsomely." The man glared at them.

"I don't have the credits or the favors, but my father does." The words were ash in Meda's mouth, but she was clawing for anything to get them out of this room.

That gave their captor pause. Vorok's grip tightened on her even further, but Meda pulled out of it and stood. Their captor kept his blaster trained on Vorok, having identified the true threat. "Kronos and your father's interests are aligned," he said.

How far had news of her unwanted engagement spread? It didn't matter. Meda had to talk fast and make up something even faster. "Not anymore. Daddy called it off." She let a little of the spoiled brat tone she heard from others in the Silver District slip into her words. She'd never called her father daddy in her life, but who would know that? "Mr. Moretti tried to kidnap me off the street! That's why I ran. This big lug said he'd take me back home, that we had to lay low for a bit until the coast was clear. He promised!" It came out a whine.

Their captor seemed to consider this. "You're saying—oof!"

Meda slammed into him, and the blaster went flying. In a perfect world, she would have managed to completely take out their captor, but he grabbed hold of her arm and pinned her to the wall in the blink of an eye.

Spittle landed on her ear as he got close. "You'll pay for that, you little—oof!" The hand holding her fell away, and Meda heard a sickening crunch before the man fell to the floor.

She looked down at him and didn't think his neck should be hanging at that angle. "Is he …," she trailed off and looked at Vorok, who's tusks were out as he glared down at the man.

"Do you really want to know, princess?" her orc asked.

No, she decided. Kidnappers didn't get her pity. "We need to go," she said.

Vorok opened the door and checked the hallway. "Looks clear."

No guard outside could mean that there were guards waiting somewhere else. Or it could mean there were no guards at all. Had their captor been working alone? Maybe he'd paid off the bikers to bring them to him. A greedy man might think he could handle the two of them until Kronos Moretti arrived.

But multiple men had kidnapped her. And it would have taken multiple men to take down Vorok. Meda wasn't letting her guard down.

They were almost to the end of the hallway, just about to pass the last door before the exit. Vorok paused, then he pushed the door open and ducked in. Meda wasn't about to wait in the hallway, so she followed him. It was an office, possibly their captor's. Papers were strewn all over the place, and there was a lock box sitting in the middle of the desk.

Vorok tried to open it, but it was locked. The lock was no match for orc strength, and he wrenched it open with a screech of metal on metal followed by an abrupt snap as the lock gave way. He looked at the contents and a laugh rumbled out of him.

Credit sticks. A whole pile of credit sticks.

He took a handful and shoved them at Meda, who put them in her pockets. Then he stuffed his pockets full too. There were still dozens in the box, but neither had more room to carry them. Vorok flipped the lid closed again, and they were off.

The exit led to stairs rather than outside, and at the bottom level, their luck ran out. She heard voices, orcish voices. Vorok was a good fighter, and he had the blaster stuffed in the waistband of his pants, but could he fight multiple orcs at once?

He didn't seem too worried.

"Trust me, princess," he whispered with his hand on the doorknob.

"I do." It felt like a vow.

"Then stay close." He pushed the door open just a sliver and roared.

The orcs snapped to attention. Meda could see just a bit around Vorok's shoulder, but it was enough. Some of them held wicked looking knives. Some held blasters. One held a thick metal chain. Too many of them to fight.

"That asshole is dead," Vorok yelled. "He came at us alone, and I killed him."

Well, that answered that. Meda didn't feel too bad about it.

A few of the orcs lowered their weapons just a bit. One sat down and picked his drink back up. Not so eager to fight when they weren't getting paid.

"I have a box full of credits right here. It's all yours if you let us walk out of here." Vorok shook the box so they could hear just how many credit sticks were in there. Hopefully no one noticed her and Vorok's full pockets.

The orc with the chain was the one who spoke. "Why don't we just kill you and take the credits?" He had a high-pitched, whiny voice, but the other orcs were nodding along.

Vorok handed her the credit box and grabbed the blaster, shooting at the floor through the cracked opening of the door. "Let's be civil. I can hurt some of you, maybe kill some of you, before you take me down. Or you get the money, and we walk out of here."

"Give us the money and the girl," the orc with the chain countered.

Vorok shot his blaster again, and this time the shot landed right at that orc's feet. "Not a chance."

"I like a fight." The orc stalked two steps closer before a different orc got in his way and punched him in the gut. The orc with the chain doubled over.

"How many credits?" the second orc asked.

"I didn't count. A bunch. And he might have more up in his office. These were on his desk in the open. We didn't take time to look around." Vorok kept the blaster trained on the orcs and looked ready to shoot. Was there any chance he could take them all out?

She didn't think the blaster was modified to be lethal, and without that, they didn't stand a chance.

The second orc laid his knife down on the table. The rest of the orcs did the same except for the one with the chain, who was still on the ground. "If Geary was stupid enough to get dead, I don't see why I should keep you. Hand over the credits and get out."

"We hand over the credits when we're at the door." Vorok holstered the blaster and reached for the box. Meda handed it back.

There was a dramatic sigh. "So untrusting. Fine. At the door." The orc crossed his arms. "Come on out."

Vorok took a deep breath and pushed the door fully open. He stepped into the makeshift bar. It looked like a warehouse of some kind, but the orcs had several bottles of alcohol sitting on a table behind them, and they'd set up tables and chairs to give themselves somewhere to sit.

Meda and Vorok passed the orcs on the way to the exit. She could hear traffic outside. They were so close. And all it would take was one jumpy orc for this to go completely wrong.

Meda was ready for it. She expected it. She'd fight until the last and hope they killed her. Anything was better than falling into the hands of Kronos Moretti.

But they made it to the exit door. Meda tested the handle. Unlocked.

Vorok chucked the box of credits straight into the middle of the orcs, and the two of them passed through the door and took off running.

It looked like they were in the heart of Nocturna,

or at least one of the livelier districts. She saw bars and clubs and dancers smoking in alleys. And people doing other stuff in alleys, too. Apparently, the alleys of Nocturna were just as well loved as the alleys of Crimson Enclave.

They didn't slow down for several blocks, but eventually they had to. Running would bring more attention to them after awhile.

And none of the orcs were chasing them.

Meda needed to take a minute to get her breath back. Then she put her hand on Vorok's shoulder. "Let's go explore the universe. I want you to come with me."

He didn't stop her from asking this time. Instead, he leaned down and kissed her right there on the street where anyone could see. They were both grinning when he pulled away.

That was answer enough.

CHAPTER 9

THEY HAD SO MANY CREDITS. Meda had ten sticks in each of her pockets, each of them filled with five thousand credits. Vorok had even more, though some of his only had a thousand credits.

Only.

She might have been a pampered princess of the Silver District, but she'd never seen so much ready cash before. Her ship to Nebula Outpost had already departed, but that didn't matter now that she had money to go anywhere she wanted.

With exactly who she wanted.

Tropicalia was supposed to be a planet dedicated to relaxation and pleasure. And in ten days, she and Vorok would find out exactly what that meant. But first, they had to get situated on their ship.

They'd booked the premier suite. It wasn't the

nicest option on their ship, but it was better by far than the single seat fare she'd managed the last time. But they were still on a spaceship, and space was limited, no matter how luxurious the room.

And that luxury came mostly in the bed.

They didn't have any luggage to store. Her bag had disappeared somewhere while she was kidnapped, and so had Vorok's. But clothes could be purchased on the ship.

And, frankly, she didn't care too much about clothes right now.

Vorok was staring at the bed like he was trying to solve a puzzle. "You don't … We' don't …" He looked between her and the bed and sounded a bit like a blushing maiden.

Meda pulled her top off and threw it aside. Vorok made a rumbling sound deep in his chest. "I want you," she said. "Here. Now. In the future. All of it. Got it?" Maybe it was sudden, but she'd never been more certain of something in her life.

Vorok opened his mouth and closed it twice, breathing heavily. He grunted again. And finally managed one word. "Mate."

Heat sizzled through her. It hadn't been real the last time, even with the orgasms. This was just for the two of them. And she wasn't quite sure what it meant to be an orc's mate, but she'd come this far already.

Meda let her pants fall to the floor and stepped out of them. She'd already removed her shoes, so that left her bare to the orc. "Take me, then."

Vorok didn't need any more encouragement. He shed his clothes, and Meda had the briefest moment to admire his green skin and the hard lines of his muscles before he swept her up into his arms and deposited her on the bed. She could take her time to look later. Right now, she needed to touch. To taste.

She reached for his cock, and he growled, stopping her. "Not yet, princess. I want to taste you first." He slid down the bed, his huge body taking up most of the space, and buried his face between her legs.

Meda arched off the bed and gasped as Vorok licked a stripe up her folds. His tusks brushed her inner thighs, and Meda shuddered at the sensation. His tongue delved inside of her. Had it always been that long? Had she just not noticed? He teased her mercilessly, bringing her to the edge and then pulling back. Sensation overwhelmed her, building and building until Meda couldn't think, could barely breathe.

She lost track of everything except the feeling of Vorok between her legs, worshipping her with his tongue. She shattered apart, and Vorok didn't stop. He lapped up her juices, and Meda cried out as another orgasm followed the first.

It was almost too much. Her body was trembling and on edge, like she might shatter into a thousand pieces. And yet she'd never felt more invincible, like the pleasure that Vorok gave her was somehow feeding her strength.

"I need to fuck you," her orc growled, kissing his way up her body, his tusks peeking out just enough to gently scrape against her sensitized skin.

Meda spread her legs. "Please," she begged. She didn't even care how wrecked she sounded. She needed him inside her.

Vorok growled again and brushed his fingers against her entrance. She could have taken him right then, her body already relaxed and eager, but her mate wanted to take care of her.

She wasn't complaining.

He worked two fingers inside of her, stretching her slowly, and Meda groaned. It was delicious torture, and she felt empty and full at the same time. Vorok curled his fingers just right, and Meda almost came again.

"Please," she repeated, tugging at his shoulders.

"Patience, princess. We have plenty of time." He added a third finger, and Meda bucked against him.

"I'm not patient." She was a spoiled brat, and she got what she wanted. She reached until her fingers brushed against his cock and stroked. "Fuck me. Make me your mate."

Vorok stilled, but energy seemed to pulse through him. His eyes went completely black, just for a moment, and his tusks jutted out a bit farther. He was a predator, and Meda was his prey.

He lined himself up, and Meda wrapped her legs around his hips, pulling him in. Vorok groaned and thrust forward, seating himself fully inside of her in one thrust. Meda cried out as her body stretched to take him. It was delicious pressure and heat.

"Fuck," Vorok muttered, his hips rocking against hers. "You're so tight, princess. So perfect." He started thrusting, and Meda matched him, meeting him thrust for thrust. Pleasure built in her again, hot and insistent. Vorok wasn't teasing this time, wasn't drawing it out. He fucked her hard and deep, hitting that spot inside of her that sent sparks through her entire body.

Meda couldn't last. She didn't want to. Vorok's thumb brushed against her clit, and she flew apart, her orgasm taking her over. Vorok thrust once, twice more, and followed her over the edge. She could feel him spilling inside of her, and the sensation made her moan once more.

She could get addicted to this.

Vorok collapsed half on top of her, and Meda

didn't care. She'd happily carry his weight for the rest of her life. She was sticky and sweaty, and Vorok was murmuring orcish endearments against her skin.

She had no idea what any of them meant, but she was pretty sure she felt the same way.

Meda traced her fingers against Vorok's back, enjoying the feeling of his skin and the hard muscle underneath. She didn't want to move, didn't want this moment to end.

And now it didn't have to. They had ten days before they got to anywhere, and then they were free to explore every inch of the universe. Together.

"So that's what it means to be an orc's mate?" she asked with a smile, pressing a kiss to Vorok's—her mate's—naked shoulder.

He pulled her close. "That's the start of it." There was a wicked promise in his eyes.

Meda smiled even wider. "I can't wait for more."

EPILOGUE

ONE YEAR *Later*

Traveling the universe was all well and good until the money ran out. Luckily, of the two of them, Vorok actually had experience with saving and budgeting. Meda had never had to pay rent before.

Real life wasn't anything like she'd thought it would be.

They settled on Risant. It was on the edge of the Oscavian Empire, a place that had been terraformed millennia ago and where people from all over the galaxy ended up. It was nice. Peaceful. And if there were pockets of the place that resembled Crimson Enclave, Meda hadn't seen them.

Neither had Vorok.

His first instinct when it came to finding work had been to be muscle for someone who needed it.

But Meda refused to let him do that. If she thought he really wanted it, then maybe she would have come around, but there'd been a defeated look in his eyes every time he talked about busting heads.

It turned out a life of busting heads made him the perfect candidate to become a boxing teacher at one of the local gyms. He was a favorite among the children who tended to end every lesson by crawling all over him when he challenged entire classes to a fight: twelve children against one orc.

The kids always won.

Meda was taking classes at the local university and working in the library to pay her way. She wasn't sure what she might do when she finished her studies, but she had time to figure it out. And she had her orc beside her.

She had a book open on her lap when he came in the door and greeted her with a wide smile. He stalked across the room and leaned down to kiss her. "How was your day?" he asked, dipping in for a second kiss before she could answer.

She wanted to pull him down and kiss him all night. The spark between them hadn't faded in the slightest. But after a year, she could control her desires.

A little.

"I'm studying Early Oscavian Civilization. Did

you know they built pyramids bigger than most modern buildings without any sort of actual technology? They just had chisels and hammers. It sounds impossible." She'd always lived in a world of tech, and they didn't teach much about ancient civilizations on Syndica. She'd never thought of what people had done before the world opened up with space travel and electricity.

"Yeah?" he said, genuinely interested. "Tell me about it."

Vorok sat beside her on the couch and threw an arm around her shoulders. She snuggled into his giant form, right where she belonged.

Thank you for reading Rescued by the Orc Enforcer!

I'd appreciate it so much if you would consider leaving a review.

NEED A BIT MORE?

Sign up at the link below to **receive a free bonus epilogue** featuring Vorok and Meda?

Find out now!
https://katerudolph.net/index.php/orc-enforcer-bonus/

WHAT TO READ NEXT

CRUX

PRINCE CRUX IS IN A BIND.

When the Dragon King commands Crux find a mate, his days of carefree bachelorhood are over. One trip to a psychic matchmaker and he's on the path to his destiny. But it all comes screeching to a halt when he meets a human woman who lights his inner fire and makes him yearn.

She's got a pair of roller skates and an attitude.

Courtney is supposed to be putting the shambles of her life back together. Getting abducted by aliens isn't part of the plan. Neither is getting rescued by a scorchingly hot dragon that makes her think of an impossible future. But they have no chance together if they can't first escape a planet full of monsters intent on their destruction.

Get your copy

ALSO BY KATE RUDOLPH

Detyen Warrior Outcasts
Fated Mate Alien Romance
These doomed warriors were abandoned by their people and live on the edge. Their mates hold the key to their salvation.
Pick a book and jump into the action today!

Dangerous Bond
Intrepid Bond
Wayward Bond

———

Mated to the Alien
Fated Mate Alien Romance

Detyens are doomed to die young if they don't find their fated mates.

Follow along as these mated pairs fight off aliens, corrupt dictators, prejudiced humans, pirates, and more! The books can be read or listened to in any order, though some characters show up in multiple stories.

Select books available in audio.

Pick a book and jump into the action today!

Ruwen

Tyral

Stoan

Cyborg

Krayter

Kayleb

Shayn

Braxtyn

Doryan

Dekon

———

Detyen Warriors

Detya was destroyed a hundred years ago. These doomed warriors are out to find justice... and their mates.

The Detyen Warriors series brings you kick butt

heroines, alpha alien heroes, fated mates, and relationships strong enough to span the galaxy!
The entire series is also available in audio!

Soulless

Ruthless

Heartless

Faultless

Endless

Guarded by the Shifter

Werewolf. Bodyguard. Mate.
The origins of these shifters are shrouded in mystery, but they're determined to protect their mates from any harm that comes their way.
Also available in audio!

Hunting Season

On the Prowl

Stalking Magic

Wolf Cursed

Hungry for the Wolf

Wolf's Temptation

Stealing the Alpha

The thief takes what she wants, but the alpha keeps what's his…

Join shifter thief Mel as she clashes with lion alpha Luke in an explosive trilogy of two opposites who can't keep away from one another.

Also available in audio!

The Alpha Heist

Entangled with the Thief

In the Alpha's Bed

———

Alien Mates: Planet Exile

Guerran is no place for pretty human women. But these alien heroes will protect their mates!

Also available in audio!

Exile's Hunter

Exile's Adored

———

Zulir Warrior Mates

Kidnapped humans. Alien Warriors. Electric wings.
The Zulir Warrior Mates series brings you human heroines and heroes abducted from Earth who find love – and wings! – with the alien warriors who rescue them.
Also available in audio!

Synnr's Saint
Synnr's Hope
Synnr's Spark
Synnr's Kiss
Synnr's Ride

————

Dragon Brides

Dragon Princes. Fierce Women. Love.
Fated mates, fierce women, and dragon princes are ready to find their mates.

Crux
Ranger
Saber
Cipher
Storm
Drake
Asher
Knox

Flint

———

Alien Holiday Romance

Christmas… in space????
These alien holiday romances look beyond Earth's winter holidays and ring in the season across the galaxy!
Select titles available in audio.
Snowed in with the Alien Beast
The Alien's Winter Gift
The Alien Reindeer's Wild Ride
Trapped with her Alien Mate

———

Alien Outlaws

Outlaws, schemes, and love… it's all there in the Alien Outlaws series…
Andie Munster is sick of life on Ixilta, the planet she got dumped on after being abducted from Earth six years ago. And when the mysterious and dangerous Xandr shows up looking for a way off the planet,

she's half-prisoner, half-co-conspirator in a wild rush
to escape.

Rogue Alien's Escape
Rogue Alien's Woman
Rogue Alien's Secret
Rogue Alien's Legacy

———

Find more by Kate Rudolph at www.katerudolph.net

ABOUT KATE RUDOLPH

KATE RUDOLPH IS a paranormal and sci-fi romance writer who lives in Indiana. She loves writing about kick butt heroines and the steamy heroes who love them. She's been devouring romance novels since she was too young to be reading them and had to hide her books so no one would take them away. She couldn't imagine a better job in this world than writing romances and sharing them with her fellow readers.

If you enjoyed this story, please consider leaving a review.

www.ingramcontent.com/pod-product-compliance
Lightning Source LLC
Chambersburg PA
CBHW021721190726
48289CB00008B/2627